BIONICLE

Island of Doom

by Greg Farshtey

SCHOLASTIC INC.
New York Toronto London Auckland Sydney
Mexico City New Delhi Hong Kong Buenos Aires

For Belisa, with respect and admiration

No part of this publication may be reproduced, stored in a retrieval system,
or transmitted in any form or by any means, electronic, mechanical, photocopying,
recording, or otherwise, without written permission of the publisher.
For information regarding permission, write to Scholastic Inc.,
Attention: Permissions Department, 557 Broadway, New York, NY 10012.

ISBN-13: 978-0-439-74560-4
ISBN-10: 0-439-74560-8

LEGO, the LEGO logo, and BIONICLE
are trademarks of The LEGO Group. © 2006 The LEGO Group.
All rights reserved. Published by Scholastic Inc.
SCHOLASTIC and associated logos are trademarks and/or
registered trademarks of Scholastic Inc.

12 11 10 9 8 7 6 5 4   7 8 9 10 11 12/0

Printed in the U.S.A.   40
First printing, February 2006

Characters

Island of Metru Nui

THE TURAGA

Dume	Elder of Metru Nui
Nuju	
Vakama	
Nokama	Former Toa Metru and Turaga of the villages of the
Onewa	island of Mata Nui
Whenua	
Matau	

THE MATORAN

Jaller	A Ta-Matoran villager, now serving as captain of the Ta-Metru Guard
Matoro	Ko-Matoran aide to Turaga Nuju

THE TOA

Takanuva	Toa of Light
Tahu Nuva	Toa Nuva of Fire
Gali Nuva	Toa Nuva of Water
Pohatu Nuva	Toa Nuva of Stone
Onua Nuva	Toa Nuva of Earth
Lewa Nuva	Toa Nuva of Air
Kopaka Nuva	Toa Nuva of Ice

Island of Voya Nui

THE MATORAN

Garan	Onu-Matoran leader of the resistance
Balta	Ta-Matoran, able to improvise tools from anything lying around
Kazi	Ko-Matoran with many secrets
Velika	Po-Matoran inventor
Dalu	Ga-Matoran fighter
Piruk	Le-Matoran, skilled in stealth

THE PIRAKA

Zaktan	Emerald-armored leader of the Piraka
Hakann	Crimson-armored Piraka
Reidak	Ebon-armored Piraka
Avak	Tan-armored Piraka
Thok	White-armored Piraka

INTRODUCTION

Six powerful figures stood on the shore of the once-great city of Metru Nui. They were the Toa Nuva, heroes whose power and skill had defeated the darkness and allowed the Matoran to return to the place that had once been their home.

All around them, Matoran were hard at work rebuilding the city. It had been damaged centuries ago by a massive earthquake and then overrun by Rahi beasts. Most of Metru Nui was in poor shape, some of it completely ruined.

The Toa Nuva and Takanuva, Toa of Light, had spent most of the past few weeks assisting in this effort. Now they had been called away by Turaga Vakama and Turaga Nuju for a private

1

conference. From their expressions, the Toa could tell they were not about to hear good news.

Vakama led the Toa to an isolated spot where Turaga Dume was waiting for them. Dume had been living in Metru Nui, waiting for the Matoran to return, for over a thousand years. He looked at the Toa Nuva with undisguised desperation in his eyes.

"My friends, I do not know how to say this," he began. "One thousand years ago, the Great Spirit Mata Nui was struck down by treachery and cast into a deep sleep. It is said that you Toa Nuva are destined to one day awaken Mata Nui and restore light and peace to the universe."

Tahu Nuva frowned. They knew all this already. Bringing the Matoran back to Metru Nui had been the first step toward awakening the Great Spirit.

"I have studied the stars, few and dim as they now are," Dume continued, gesturing toward the darkened sky. It was true that few points of light could be seen, and those that were visible had hardly any glow. "I have consulted with Turaga Nuju, who was once a talented interpreter of the messages to be read in the heavens. He agrees with my findings."

"Which are?" Kopaka Nuva asked, impatience creeping into his voice.

"Mata Nui is not merely asleep," Dume said quietly. "My friends, Mata Nui is dying."

After the initial shock and disbelief had passed, the Toa Nuva insisted on seeing the proof of Dume's claims. He and Nuju showed them how the passages of the stars, and their diminishment in brightness and number, spoke of an end to all things. In the time that had passed since Mata Nui first fell into slumber, the Great Spirit's hold on life had gradually grown weaker. If action was not taken, he would die, and all hope for the universe would be lost.

"What can we do?" asked Gali Nuva, Toa of Water. "With all our power, there must be some way we can save Mata Nui."

"And so there is," said Dume. "There is a great Kanohi Mask of Power — the Mask of Life — hidden far from here. That mask is the key to saving the life of Mata Nui. You must travel to an island that should not exist, but does, to find this treasure."

"And when we have found it?" said Onua Nuva, Toa of Earth. "Then what?"

"It is our belief — our *hope* — that once you have the mask, the Great Spirit will find a way to tell you what to do next," said Turaga Vakama.

Tahu Nuva nodded. "This doesn't sound very hard, not compared to some of the things we have already done. We travel to this island, find this mask —"

"And quick-save the universe," finished Lewa Nuva brightly. "Just like past-old times!"

Turaga Dume shook his head. "Do not take this task lightly, Toa Nuva. The stars are there for all to see, including those with evil intent. There are some who would not weep at Mata Nui's passing . . . and others who simply wish to possess the awesome power of that mask. If they should reach its hiding place before you . . ."

Tahu turned to Gali. "Tell Takanuva: We must leave at once."

"No!" snapped Dume. The others looked at him, startled. "Takanuva must stay here."

Kopaka wheeled on the Turaga. "I don't understand. You tell us that this mission is vital, and then subtract one-seventh of our power. Why?"

"Metru Nui must be defended in your absence," Dume explained. "The stars say that it is Takanuva's destiny to remain here and guard the Matoran."

"I have to stay?" asked the Toa of Light in disbelief. "The others may need me. I should be with them!"

"You are needed here," said Turaga Vakama. "The time will come when your power may be all that stands between us and the darkness. On that day, you must be prepared to act. Until then, your place is in Metru Nui with us."

"All right, I will stay," said Takanuva. "But the others — do you think they will be all right?"

Vakama pondered for a long moment before answering. Then he said simply, "No, Takanuva. No, I do not."

# ONE

The Island of Voya Nui:

The small armored figure walked purpose-fully across the rocky landscape. His eyes scanned the ground and the steep slopes on either side, searching for the slightest sign of moisture. It was a ritual he repeated every day without fail, but one that grew more frustrating each time.

There is precious little water left, Garan thought as he studied the bone-dry terrain. *When the lake fully recedes, I don't know what we will do. Only the green belt near the coast remains lush, and none but the Great Spirit knows why.*

In the distance, the volcano rumbled and spewed red-hot lava into the air. The ground trembled beneath his feet, but Garan had long since learned to keep his balance. A Matoran

7

villager on the island of Voya Nui quickly mastered the art of dealing with eruptions, tremors, and drought, or he did not last long.

He stopped at what looked to be a likely spot. Crossing his twin tools, he fired a pulse bolt at the ground. It blasted through the rock, gaining strength as it traveled, until it dissipated about six feet down. A little puddle of stagnant water rested at the bottom of the hole.

Garan sighed and looked out at the ocean in the distance. *So much water, and none that we can drink. If only —*

His eyes caught sight of something bobbing in the surf far below. It gleamed in the bright sunlight . . . it looked like a canister of some kind. As Garan watched, it struck the ice ring that surrounded the island and ground to a halt.

The lid of the canister rotated with a hiss and then fell off, sliding across the ice and back into the water. Part of Garan wanted to run down to the shore and see what was inside, but he restrained himself. He crouched behind a boulder and watched carefully.

After a moment, a figure emerged from the canister. He was strong and lean, clad in snow-white armor that was lined with spikes. Long, muscular legs ended in two-toed feet that effortlessly gripped the ice. Strangest of all was the face, with eyes that glowed red and a smile that could best be described as savage. The figure paused and looked around with seeming satisfaction, then began walking down the path that led to the Matoran settlement.

Garan peered around the rock to keep the being in sight. The armored figure didn't look like anything he had seen before, but there was no mistaking the aura of power that surrounded him. It seemed impossible, but there was only one thing this new arrival could be — a Toa!

The white figure stopped suddenly. A Visorak was watching him from behind some nearby scrub, and evidently the Toa had detected it. Casually, as if he ran into such things every day, the Toa waved a hand in the Visorak's direction. The scrub suddenly came to life, its thick branches wrapping around the spider creature and squeezing tight. It did not let go until the Visorak had collapsed, its only movement an occasional twitch. At that point, the plant went back to being just a plant.

Garan was awestruck. With powers like that, this new Toa would be able to solve all of Voya Nui's problems in no time. He smiled happily, confident that the Matoran's old way of life would soon be just a memory.

Reidak waited impatiently inside his canister. He had felt it wash up on the shore minutes ago. Zaktan had stated that Matoran would be sure to come investigate, and when they did, he was to open the canister and declare that he was the Toa of Earth.

This, Reidak decided, sounded all too much like some of Zaktan's other plans. They always tended to be overcomplicated and too subtle for Reidak. After all, he wasn't a Toa — he was an ex–Dark Hunter and now a Piraka. He didn't even look like a Toa. All the Toa he had ever met were small and weak and usually died much too quickly. He preferred opponents with more longevity.

I have had enough of this, he grumbled to himself. *I have heard only sea birds landing on this canister. If the Matoran will not find me, I will find them, much to their regret.*

Shrugging his powerful shoulders, Reidak tore his way out of the metal canister. Brushing scraps of iron off of himself, he stalked inland.

Balta had come upon an opened canister while scouting for food. He had no idea what it might be. Perhaps Matoran from some other village had received the messages they had been throwing into the ocean and sent supplies? He knew that this was highly unlikely.

His doubts were quickly confirmed. The canister was empty. But there were footprints trailing away toward the settlement. Balta decided that food could wait. This was a mystery, after all, and Voya Nui could use a little mystery.

He caught up with the red-armored newcomer about an hour later. The first thing he noticed was the stranger's smile — at least, he thought that was supposed to be a smile. There was something about it that reminded him of a predator's grin . . . just before it pounced on prey.

Balta took a few cautious steps and called out, "Hello?"

The stranger turned around. He hesitated a moment before speaking, as if he were sizing up the Matoran. Then he said, "Do you know who I am?"

Balta shook his head.

"Well, you will," the newcomer assured him. "I am Toa Hakann. Someday, stories will be told about this day, when the Toa came to Voya Nui. Legends will be crafted that will live on long after you are gone, Matoran."

Balta wasn't sure what to say to that, and the being who called himself a Toa wasn't waiting for his response. Instead, he was pointing to a herd of Rahi beasts who were grazing on the near-barren rock.

"What are those?"

"Kikanalo," Balta answered. "They eat

plants, when they can find them. They are very big and powerful, and their stampedes are frightening . . . but they're mostly harmless."

Hakann smiled. Then he stared hard at the Kikanalo for a few seconds. Crimson bolts of energy erupted from his forehead and struck the Rahi, completely obliterating them. All that was left was a few wisps of smoke.

"And now," Hakann said, satisfied, "they are not even that."

"Why — why did you do that?" Balta sputtered, stunned. "They were no threat to anyone!"

"They were blocking my view," Hakann replied casually. "I believe it's time for you to take me to your village? After all, we have legends to create, don't we?"

Balta couldn't give any answer but yes — after all, who could deny a Toa what he wanted? But he couldn't help looking back at the charred earth where once some of the mightiest of Rahi had stood.

*   *   *

Piruk ran for his life.

Flashes of memory intruded on his panic, goading him to run even faster. He had been walking along the beach. He had spotted a canister. It had opened up and someone . . . some *thing* . . . had come out of it.

It was clad in green armor, and at first Piruk thought it must be a Toa, or some other powerful entity come to help Voya Nui. But the newcomer had regarded him coldly, like he was a rockworm ready for dissection. When the figure spoke, it sounded like many voices hastily joined into one. Worst of all, his body seemed to be shifting, as if it was not a cohesive whole but a random collection of parts constantly changing position. Terrified, Piruk fled.

Unfortunately, he just wasn't fast enough. He could hear something following him, but it wasn't the sound of someone running in pursuit. It was more like a low hum that grew louder and louder all the time.

A cloud passed over him, and for a moment, he could not see. Then suddenly the green figure was standing in front of him, holding out an armored hand.

"Do not . . . be afraid," the stranger hissed. "Toa Zaktan. Here to help."

Piruk didn't believe this for a minute. He had never met a Toa in person, but he had heard plenty about them. None of the tales spoke of anything even remotely like this strange being. Toa were courageous, heroic, and reassuring figures. *And this thing could give a lava eel nightmares,* Piruk thought to himself.

"All right. I'm not afraid," he lied. "But, um, we really don't need any help. Everything's fine here. Maybe you could find some other island to protect? Please?"

Zaktan shook his head. The movement produced a strange rustling noise, almost like dry leaves caught in a gust of wind.

"Toa Zaktan," the figure repeated. "Here to help."

Piruk looked into the eyes of the stranger. There was no warmth or regard there.

"Then stay here," Piruk said. "Stay right

here, and . . . and don't move. I will go find some other Matoran who would know how you could help. Okay?"

Before Zaktan could answer, Piruk took off for the settlement. This time, he didn't hear the hum behind him, just the sounds of his feet hitting the ground and the breath exploding from his lungs. He wouldn't slow down until he reached home.

Avak scowled as he hauled the canister up onto the icy beach. Vezok was supposed to have been here to help, but he was nowhere to be found. As usual, he was off somewhere pursuing his own plans and ignoring the needs of the team.

This is the most important job, he reminded himself. *Far more vital than fooling a handful of Matoran into thinking we're Toa, because I doubt we will fool them for long. No, the crystal inside this canister is the key to everything.*

Avak paused. He was absolutely certain of the truth of what he had just said, but one thing still bothered him. He wasn't sure *why* he was so certain. The others were too consumed with finding the treasure here to pay any attention to questions or doubts. Avak was different. He knew to listen to his inner voices.

That is why I will still be alive, with the treasure, when the others are no more, he thought, tapping his head with an armored finger. *Because of what I have up here.*

Vezok waded toward shore. His canister had developed a leak halfway to Voya Nui, and when he tried to open it, he found that it was welded shut. Fortunately, he had enough raw strength to punch his way out. That didn't change the fact that one of his teammates had tried to make sure he was lost at sea. It wasn't hard to guess who.

Cunning. Devious. Insane, he said to himself. *Hakann. Has to be.*

He didn't give in to rage or bellow threats. Instead, he calmly made his way through the water, his eyes fixed on the volcano erupting on the island up ahead. He idly wondered if the Matoran had any idea what was hidden on their little piece of rock.

Probably not, he decided. *But they will help us find it just the same. And once we do, we will plan our next steps — after, of course, I have twisted Hakann's head so far around he can stare himself in the eye.*

The thought brought his first smile of the day.

 **TWO**

Turaga Dume led the Toa Nuva and the other Turaga down a musty, narrow tunnel beneath the surface of Metru Nui.

"Where are we going?" asked Tahu Nuva.

"Patience," Dume replied.

Gali Nuva smiled. Asking Tahu to have patience was like asking a raging fire to please not be so very hot. The Toa Nuva of Fire started to say something back, but Turaga Vakama shook his head no.

Whenua looked around. They were already well beneath the ruins of the Archives, the maintenance tunnels, and anyplace else any Matoran had ever been. *If we keep going like this, we are going to come out on the other side of the world,* he said to himself.

Turaga Dume ducked his head to walk through a low entrance. The Toa Nuva had to get down on their bellies and crawl through the same opening.

"How did you ever seek-find this place?" asked Lewa Nuva, Toa of Air. "And why?"

"I didn't spend the last thousand years playing with puzzle stones or making a dictionary of chute speak, Lewa," Dume replied. "I spent it preparing for your eventual return."

"All this for us?" asked Lewa, glancing at the rough-hewn, damp rock walls that seemed to close in on them. "You shouldn't have. Really."

"Enough," said Dume. "We're here."

The Toa Nuva crawled out of the tunnel and got to their feet. "Here" turned out to be a massive chamber that was obviously not a natural structure. It was almost a perfect sphere, with the entrances to six passageways on the far wall. The chamber was dominated by a pool of liquid protodermis in the center, but what attracted the Toa's attention was what was floating in the center of that pool.

Six cylinders bobbed in the water, small

red lights flashing on their sides. They looked almost exactly like the cylinders that had first brought the Toa to the island of Mata Nui. How they had wound up in them or ended up in the waters around the island was still unclear. But they now knew that they had spent perhaps a thousand years floating in the ocean in those canisters before finally being summoned to the island.

"Oh, no," said Pohatu Nuva, taking a step backward. "I'm not getting into one of those things again. I remember what happened the last time. . . . Well, I don't remember, really, but I'm not up for sleeping another thousand years."

"What is this place?" Kopaka Nuva asked, ignoring the Toa of Stone. "Is this where we came from originally on our journey above?"

"Not here," said Dume. "But perhaps someplace very much like it."

"That makes no sense," said Onua. "I recall the legend — we were said to have fallen to Mata Nui from the heavens."

Dume nodded and smiled. "Indeed. And if

you were shot into the sky over your island, only to plunge back down into the ocean . . . you would have fallen from the heavens, would you not?"

Onua frowned. Once again, everything he had thought he knew about his past had been turned on its head. He hated when that happened.

"Why have you brought us here?" Gali Nuva asked. "What is the point of showing us this?"

It was Turaga Vakama who answered. "The island that hides the Mask of Life is located up above, in the same ocean in which Mata Nui floats. It is many kio south of our former home, so far away that none of us ever suspected its existence."

"The journey overland and by water to reach it would be dangerous, most likely fatal," Turaga Nokama added. "We believe these canisters are the only safe way for you to reach your destination."

"And what is our destination?" asked Kopaka Nuva. "What is this remote place that conceals a Kanohi mask of such power?"

"The stars call it Voya Nui," said Turaga Dume. "But they have another name for it as well: 'the daggers of Death.' I fear the second name may be more accurate."

"Well, there is one good thing," said the Toa Nuva of Air. "With a happy-cheer name like that, I doubt the place is very crowded."

Balta crouched on a rock, watching Avak work. The brown figure had been mining minerals all day and then cleaving them together with one solid strike of his tool. Balta had no idea what he was making, but the process was certainly interesting.

"Is that some kind of new machine?" he asked finally. "Something to help us find water?"

"Right. That's just what it is," Avak answered without looking up. "Once this is done, you won't have to worry about water, or anything else, anymore."

Balta hopped down from the boulder and peered closer at Avak's handiwork. "What's that do?" he asked, pointing to an unfamiliar component. "And what's that? How do those two pieces join together? Is that the only color that piece comes in? I think it would look better in a different shade of gray."

The Matoran wasn't quite sure just what happened next. One second, everything was normal, and the next he was inside a cell made of some sort of clear, metallic substance. He could see out, but when he tried to speak, no sound escaped his mouth.

"Matoran should be seen, and not heard," Avak growled. "And even 'seen' is debatable."

Without another word, he went back to his work, ignoring the muted cries of the Matoran.

The white-armored figure, who called himself Thok, had spent much of the day testing his powers. While Garan tried to get some information on where he had come from and why, Thok busied himself bringing rocks and trees to a semblance of life and making them battle each other.

"How did you know we needed help?" asked Garan, hoping he wasn't being too annoying.

"I'm a Toa, aren't I?" Thok replied. "Knowing things is part of my job, along with imposing my idea of peace and order on others and unleashing elemental powers on anyone who disagrees with me." He paused, then quickly added, "More knowing things, though. Now it's your turn. Why are you here? What keeps Matoran on such a barren rock?"

"This is my home," Garan answered. "A thousand years ago or so, we were part of a much larger landmass. Then there was a quake, an explosion, and our portion of the continent broke loose and rocketed upward. Many good friends died that day. Those of us who survived were determined to make a life here in their memory."

"Very noble. Very moving," Thok said quietly. "And, of course, I don't believe a word."

Garan was too shocked to reply. Thok continued, "There are only two good reasons for you to have stayed on Voya Nui all this time, scratching and clawing for bare existence: One, you're too cowardly to try to escape; or two . . .

you're hiding something. There's a treasure on this island and you don't want to leave it behind. That's the truth, little Matoran, isn't it?"

"No!" cried Garan. "Treasure? On this island? You've been reading the wrong legends."

Thok's eyes narrowed and his smile turned into a snarl. Garan took a step back. "I'm sorry, but if there was a treasure here, I would know, wouldn't I?"

"Yes," said Thok, leaning in close. "You *would* know. That is exactly the point."

The Matoran decided to change the subject. "What kind of a Kanohi mask do you wear, Toa Thok? I have never seen one, um, shaped quite like that."

The armored figure smiled. "I am not wearing a mask."

"Oh," said Garan, confused. "I thought all Toa wore Kanohi masks."

Thok's chilling grin grew broader. "Now why would I ever want to cover up this face?"

* * *

Dalu walked purposefully down the shore. Up ahead, Vezok sat cross-legged on the rocks, gazing up at a tall, skeletal tree. She hated to disturb him when he was apparently deep in meditation, but there were many things she needed to ask. As a Toa of Water, he would certainly have the inner strength and sense of balance to be able to help her.

"I'm sorry to intrude, Toa Vezok," Dalu began. "But I need some advice. You see, I have a terrible temper. . . . Garan says I erupt worse than the volcano. I don't know that I am that bad, although I did get a little irritated last week and smash a rock wall . . . with my head . . . still, that's no reason to —"

Vezok held up a hand. "Be still. The others fear your anger, but you should not. If they are too weak to stand up to you, then that means you are meant to command them. Seize control from your Turaga. Take over the island. Then come see me when you're done."

Dalu thought her ears were playing tricks

on her: She expected Vezok to counsel contem-
plation and reasoned discussion, not a grab for
power. What kind of a Toa was he?

"Well, we don't have a Turaga," she replied.
"He was killed when the island was blown loose
of the mainland. We just look after ourselves."

"Good," Vezok said, never taking his eyes
off the tree. "Turaga are always getting under-
foot, anyway. I remember one I met a long time
ago. I wanted to do something. He kept saying
no. We ended up having a discussion about per-
sonal destiny."

"What happened?"

Vezok glanced at her and bared his teeth in
a wolfish grin. "Turned out he didn't have as
much time to achieve his as he thought."

That was enough for Dalu, who began to
back up the way she had come. Maybe she and
Garan were not the best of friends all the time,
but he had to be made aware of this. She wasn't
sure if all the legends she had heard about Toa
were just wrong, or if these particular Toa had
simply gone mad on their journey to Voya Nui.

But something was chilling her, and it wasn't the ocean breeze coming across the ice.

"Well, thanks for the advice," she said hurriedly. "I'll certainly think about it."

"I have one more piece of advice for you, Matoran," Vezok said. "You and your friends really shouldn't go wandering around this dangerous island, asking strangers a lot of questions and worrying about things that don't concern you."

His eyes glowed red for the briefest of instants. Something slammed into Dalu, knocking her off her feet. She hit the ground hard, the breath driven from her lungs.

Vezok rose and started walking away. "You might get hurt."

THREE

Life had changed on Voya Nui, and Garan was not at all sure what to make of it.

In the days since Thok, Reidak, Hakann, Zaktan, Avak, and Vezok had arrived, they had transformed the island to their liking with the help of the Matoran. Two teams of villagers, led by Dalu and Kazi, had been put to work drilling holes in the side of the volcano to allow the lava to flow out. Piruk and Balta were overseeing teams assigned to dig vast reservoirs to collect the lava. None of this made much sense to Garan. Voya Nui's problem was a lack of water, and they could not drink molten lava or the rock it hardened into.

The strangest project of all was Velika's. His group of Matoran had been put to work building a massive structure in the center of the island under the supervision of Toa Avak. They had already been informed that, once it was completed, no Matoran would ever be allowed to enter.

The whole situation disturbed Garan greatly. Since arriving, the Toa had done nothing toward alleviating the drought or aiding in the defense against dangerous Rahi. They had either ignored requests for help on various matters or else postponed dealing with them indefinitely. While they had not done any harm to a Matoran, so far as he knew, they had also shown no patience with slow or clumsy workers. Some Toa, like Zaktan, seemed to want to avoid the Matoran as much as possible.

"This is not how Toa should behave," Garan muttered to himself.

"And you, of course, are an expert on that."

Garan jumped at the sound of the voice behind him. He turned to see Hakann standing there, a nasty smile plastered on his face.

"You have seen Toa in a crisis before," Hakann continued, his tone smooth and dangerous. "You know just how they should handle matters."

"No, that's not what I —"

Hakann grabbed Garan by the throat and lifted him into the air, still smiling all the while. "Why don't you do your job, Matoran, and let us do ours? Hmmmm?"

He gently put Garan on his shoulder. The Matoran wanted desperately to jump off, but he feared what would happen if he did. "Now, over there, we will build the temple," said Hakann, pointing to a rocky peak. "I think that will be just about perfect."

The area Hakann indicated was one of the few inland areas of the island that supported any vegetation. A thick bed of flowering plants some- how managed to survive the hostile terrain and flourish, much to the delight of the Rahi who came there to feed.

"Of course, we will have to be rid of all that shrubbery," Hakann said. His eyes glowed a bright red and a second later the plant life was ablaze. Garan felt his heart sink.

"Now it is ready for the temple," Hakann announced, satisfied.

"A temple? A temple dedicated to what?"

"To the three things that matter most in my life," Hakann answered solemnly. "The three things I consider first before taking any action."

Garan had no idea what he might be referring to, but decided to give the Toa the benefit of the doubt. "Unity, duty, and destiny?" he suggested, naming the three virtues that guided Matoran life.

"No, no," Hakann laughed. "Me, myself, and I."

Metru Nui had been abandoned for many centuries, and it looked it. Wreckage from the earthquake a millennium ago was still strewn everywhere, and it had to be cleared before the Matoran could begin work rebuilding their city.

Jaller had been leading these efforts in Ta-Metru for some days. He had grown accustomed to the sight of Turaga Vakama and Turaga Dume watching over the work, while Tahu Nuva used his flame power to melt rubble into slag. Now, though, both the Turaga and the Toa Nuva were conspicuous by their absence. The rumor was that this was the case all over the city.

Puzzled and worried, Jaller had traveled to Ko-Metru to see if anyone there had heard anything. He was surprised to spot Matoro hard at work overseeing the repair of a Knowledge Tower. As Turaga Nuju's aide and translator, Matoro was always with the elders.

Jaller wasted no time. "Where are they?"

"Who?" said Matoro, not taking his eyes off his task.

"The Turaga. The Toa Nuva. No one has seen them today, and whenever they vanish like that, it means trouble is coming. Now where are they, and why aren't you with them, Matoro?"

The Ko-Matoran turned to his friend. Jaller recognized the look in his eyes. It meant Matoro had learned something at one of the Turaga councils and was forbidden to speak of it. "If I tell you what I know, I will violate my oath," Matoro said. "If I tell you I know nothing, I will be lying to my friend. You can imagine how enthusiastic I am about having this choice to make. I'm sorry, Jaller, I can't give you an answer."

Jaller patted Matoro on the shoulder. "All right. But in this case, old friend, not giving an answer *is* giving an answer. There is danger the Toa must face — and whatever they confront inevitably comes after us, too. I need to find out what's going on."

Matoro shrugged. "I can't imagine who you can ask."

Jaller smiled and gestured toward the coast with his crafter's tool. "Oh, I do. You like riddles, Matoro . . . try this one. What's white and gold and can't keep a secret to save his life?"

"Takanuva!"

The Toa of Light turned to see Jaller approaching him. The Ta-Matoran was riding Pewku, the Ussal crab that had once been Takanuva's pet. After becoming a Toa, Takanuva had given Pewku to his best friend.

"Jaller! I thought you would be busy

rebuilding the Great Furnace one brick at a time, or polishing the Archives," the Toa of Light chuckled. "Instead you're not working and you're here . . . and . . . ," Takanuva's smile faded. "This can't be good, can it?"

"No, but it can be quick," said the Ta-Matoran. "Where are the Toa Nuva?"

Takanuva thought for a long time. Then he said, "All right, I guess you should know. In fact, I know you should. We just got finished hearing all the secrets of the Turaga's past, and now they are keeping Matoran in the dark again. I won't stand for that."

Jaller reached out and shook the hand of the Toa of Light. "Then let's go tell them together."

Garan sat alone on a rocky peak that afforded an excellent view of the entire island. He had been wandering around, troubled, since his encounter with Hakann. It now seemed the Matoran needed help to save them from the Toa, he thought bleakly.

He spotted Dalu climbing up the slope. He knew instantly that something was very wrong, for he had never before seen her looking afraid.

"We have to talk," she said as she reached the summit. "And I hope it's not already too late."

Avak gently tapped two pieces of metal into place, then stood back to admire his work. From bits and pieces salvaged from the canisters, he had constructed a handheld tool that would give the Piraka complete mastery of this island. Now, he just had to make five more, one for each of —

Or do I? he suddenly thought. *Zaktan might say he wants everyone equipped, but what can he really do about it if I say no?*

Then he remembered a night long ago, an island far to the south, and a Toa of Plasma who didn't beg quite loud enough or share quite enough information. Zaktan had dragged the Toa off. Less than two minutes later, the Piraka leader returned alone. When Avak went to check on the situation, all he could find of the Toa were bits of armor, a mask that looked half-devoured, and puddles of something Avak preferred not to try and identify.

Five more, he decided abruptly. *Sure. I can do that.*

He glanced to the west. The Matoran had already finished building the stronghold. He and Vezok had successfully installed the crystal collection sphere under Zaktan's watchful eye. It hadn't been easy to get the Matoran to work diligently on something that had no connection to the problems they were having here, but the suggestion that there were far worse jobs — for example, polishing the ice ring around the island by hand — seemed to spur them on.

Avak turned back to his work just in time to see a Matoran scurrying away. He thought it might be Velika, although he really couldn't be bothered to keep their names straight. What was the Matoran up to? Spying?

That would present a problem. If he told Zaktan the Matoran were getting suspicious, the Piraka leader would want them all eliminated.

That would mean no labor force, and therefore a lot more work for the other Piraka.

No, better I should just handle this myself, he decided. *Maybe a quick swim in the lava will teach our curious friend to mind his own business.*

Avak rose and started after the Matoran, trying to decide whether "medium" would be enough to teach Velika his mistake, or if he should go right for "well done." He never saw Garan and Kazi emerge from the rocks, grab the tool he had just completed, and run off with it.

The rebellion had begun.

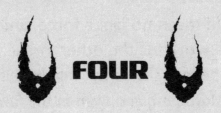 **FOUR**

Takanuva and Jaller emerged from the tunnel to see the seven Turaga standing alone. There was no sign of the Toa Nuva, only six empty cradles where once the canisters had rested.

"Where?" asked Jaller.

"Someplace far too dangerous for any Matoran to go," Turaga Dume answered. "This is a matter for Toa."

Jaller threw his crafter's tool on the ground in anger. "That's not good enough!"

"Jaller!" Vakama exclaimed, shocked.

"We are not little Rahi that need to be looked after," the Ta-Matoran said quietly. "We fought the Rahi, the Bohrok, and the Bohrok Va. We stood up to the Rahkshi — I *died* in that struggle! The Matoran need your guidance and

your wisdom, but not to be coddled, protected . . . or lied to."

An uncomfortable silence followed.
Takanuva looked down at the floor. Vakama
glanced at Dume, who looked furious. Jaller looked
from one Turaga to another, waiting for one of
them to start talking. When none of them did, he
kicked his tool, sending it skidding across the
stone to stop at Dume's feet.

"All right. When you are ready to treat the
Matoran with respect, let us know. Until then,
no one is doing any more work. Metru Nui was
in ruins for a thousand years . . . another thousand won't hurt."

Jaller turned and departed, leaving behind
eight very disturbed figures.

"What is it?" Kazi asked.

Velika and Balta carefully examined the
tool stolen from Avak. It was obviously meant to
be carried or perhaps latched on to the arm.
Balta had already identified what looked like a

launching apparatus, but there did not seem to be anything to shoot.

"I don't think this is for building, or to help us find water," said Garan.

"What if they find out we took it?" Piruk asked, anxiously. He was in no hurry to run into Zaktan again.

"Dalu is outside watching the approach to the cave," Balta assured him. "If she sees one of them coming, she will let us know." He turned to Velika. "What do you think?"

"When the Kanohi dragon roars, do not look for the stone rat," the Po-Matoran replied. The others waited for him to explain just what that saying meant, but Velika added nothing.

"I hate it when he does that," said Kazi.

"It's obvious," said Garan impatiently. "If you hear one Rahi, don't expect a different one to appear. If the signs all point one way, then don't expect the truth to be something else."

"Oh. That clears everything up," Kazi said sarcastically.

"It's not a tool, not like the kind we use," Garan explained. "It's a weapon. The question is: What do they need it for? Who is there here to fight?"

Balta hesitated a moment, before saying quietly, "Us?"

"But . . . but they're Toa!" Piruk insisted.

"Are they?" asked Garan. "I'm not so sure. Not sure at all."

Dalu spotted Avak heading for the cave. She crossed her tools and felt a surge of energy go through them. The next instant, Avak was rocketing forward at super-speed. Unprepared for the sudden acceleration, he stumbled and flew headlong into a pile of rocks.

Dalu separated the tools and took a deep breath. Each time she used her equipment to temporarily enhance someone else's attributes, it drained some of her own energy. She knew what would result if she used the tools too often in a short span of time: unconsciousness and probably death. But she had already decided she would risk whatever she had to in order to keep Avak from finding the others.

Avak had shaken off the impact and gotten to his feet, leaning on a boulder for support. Dalu sent another jolt of power to him, this time aimed at enhancing his strength. The boulder suddenly crumbled to pieces before his might and Avak almost fell again. Frustrated, he kicked out at the rock pile, his blow turning a thousand pounds of rock into a cloud of dust.

Dalu fought the wave of dizziness that washed over her. She had one more thing to try — a more potent attack than the others, but its use almost guaranteed she would collapse from the power drain. Hopefully, it would be enough to convince Avak to turn back.

She crossed her tools for a third time. This jolt of power targeted Avak's hearing, enhancing it well beyond normal levels. He stopped dead as his mind was suddenly assailed by every noise on the island. He could hear the breathing of every living thing, every rock being struck by a tool, every Rahi's cry, the sizzle of lava, even every pebble that scraped against another. It was overwhelming, maddening.

Then, as suddenly as it had begun, it was over. He staggered forward a few steps, then stopped and turned around. Someone or something was doing this to him, of that he had no doubt, but he was in no condition to search for it. *Let Reidak do it,* he thought. *That's what the big mass of muscle is for, after all.*

He started back down the path, never knowing that his opponent was a Ga-Matoran who now lay among the rocks, as still as death.

"So, what do we do?" asked Kazi. "We're Matoran. They're To — whatever it is they are. Vezok bites boulders in half for fun. Hakann keeps turning Rahi into piles of ash. Reidak slipped and fell 800 feet, smashed into the ice ring head-first, and all it did was make him irritable. I can't say I like our chances."

Garan nodded. "Maybe not. But we need

to know what's going on here. We need someone to get close to that stronghold they had us
build. Avak and Vezok have been moving equipment in there for days. Someone has to go in
there, someone they won't look twice at. . . ."

As one, they turned and looked at Piruk.

After several minutes of whispered argument, they convinced the Le-Matoran to take the
job. Garan sent Balta out to find Dalu and tell her
the meeting was over and that they were heading
back to the settlement. When he returned, Balta's
expression was grim.

"You all better come," he said. "I've never
seen her this bad."

Zaktan stood in the vast collection chamber. The
vaulted room was bare save for a huge crystal
sphere in the center. As the emerald-hued being
watched, green and black smoke slowly began to
fill the sphere. His eyes glowed as the smoke
became denser and more viscous, bolts of elec-
tricity crackling in the midst of its substance.

The others believe all this equipment is just

another tool to be used in obtaining the Mask of Life, Zaktan thought. *They have no concept of what it is really for, nor will they until it is far too late.*

"Soon," he whispered in a multitude of voices. "When the gathering is complete and the mask has been found . . ."

In a heavily shadowed corner, Piruk listened, paralyzed with fear. Slipping into the building past Reidak had been bad enough. Finding this horror inside was enough to make him want to turn around and tell Garan to do his own information gathering.

"Life from death," the armored figure breathed. "Death from life."

And me a long way from here, Piruk decided, edging toward the exit. He had made it halfway there when the door suddenly burst open and Hakann and Avak marched into the room. Zaktan whirled at the unexpected interruption.

"You were not summoned!" he hissed.

"The Matoran are getting restless," Hakann replied. "If you weren't spending all your time in here, you would know that. Then again, if you were spending time with them, they would have skipped 'restless' and gone straight to 'panic.' You don't exactly inspire warm feeling."

"One of the zamor launchers was stolen," Avak broke in. "When I tried to track it down, I was attacked by —"

"By a Matoran," Hakann said, smiling. "Great and powerful Avak was beaten by a Matoran. What would our old friends among the Dark Hunters say about that?"

"They're going to be reciting your eulogy if you don't shut up," Avak growled. "Zaktan, this plan is not going to work. And if they catch on, we will have hundreds of angry Matoran swarming all around like insects . . ."

Zaktan shot him an icy look. Avak immediately realized what he had said wrong. Zaktan's body was an aggregate of trillions of microscopic creatures called protodites, each containing a portion of his consciousness. This gave him unusual powers, but it also created an aura so alien that not even his allies liked being around him. The protodites shifted position in waves, causing his body to be in constant motion, a sight that was nauseating if one looked long enough.

"The plan is not at fault," said Zaktan. "The failure is *yours*. You were supposed to act like Toa so the Matoran would not suspect the truth."

"Well, we're *not* Toa!" Avak snapped. "We're Piraka. Thieves, killers, and, once we have the Mask of Life, rulers. The Toa couldn't stop us, the Dark Hunters couldn't keep us in line, and maybe the days of taking orders from you are over, too."

Piruk had to stifle a gasp. Garan had been right. The island was under the control of six brutal maniacs who thought of Matoran as insects. They were searching for this "Mask of Life," whatever that might be, and somehow he doubted they would leave peacefully once they had it.

His worrying was interrupted by an angry hum that filled the chamber. Zaktan's right arm had extended toward Avak, and a swarm of protodites now engulfed the brown Piraka. Normally, the creatures were too small to be seen by the naked eye, but in the trillions they made up a greenish mass that writhed like a tentacle. Avak hit the floor and rolled as the swarm flew into his eyes. Hakann made no move to help, just stood by and watched as if it were all staged for his entertainment.

Avak fought a growing sense of horror. The protodites didn't sting, but their sheer numbers threatened to suffocate him. He opened his mouth to scream, only to have the tiny creatures swarm into it. A cloud of green threatened to be the last thing he would ever see.

Hakann glanced at Zaktan. "When you're quite finished?"

Zaktan gave no sign he had heard, but withdrew the protodites back to him. They slowly coalesced back into his right arm, although Hakann guessed it was with some reluctance. These days, Zaktan so rarely let them out to play.

Avak remained on the floor, coughing.

Zaktan walked over and nudged him with his foot. "Next time, I will not be so merciful," the green Piraka said flatly.

"You can take your 'mercy' and —" Avak began, ready to spring to the attack.

Hakann stepped in between them before a fight could break out. "What Avak means is that he is grateful for your understanding. He spoke out of turn and deeply regrets it. Don't you, Avak?"

When Avak didn't answer, Hakann snapped his foot back and kicked the brown Piraka in the side. "*Don't you,* Avak?" he repeated.

"Yes," Avak spat. "I'm starting to regret a lot of things."

Hakann turned his attention back to Zaktan. "The Matoran think they have reason to fear us. I suggest we give them something to really be afraid of."

As Zaktan smiled his approval, Piruk slipped out of the chamber. The Matoran had to be warned that everything they had gone through up to now had been a game of slides and shadows compared to what was about to take place.

If only there were Toa here, he thought as he slipped past Reidak. *Real Toa. But who am I kidding? Even if there were any coming, by the time they get here . . . they'll only be in time to bury us.*

FIVE

Two dozen Matoran labored in the hot afternoon sun. For days now, they had been digging channels to allow the lava to flow from the volcano into vast reservoirs. It was hard and confusing work. They couldn't understand why the Toa would want the lava drained from inside the mountain. Some of the wittier Matoran started calling their daily chore "lava farming."

"How much longer are we going to have to do this?" asked one.

"Until there's no more lava left?" suggested his companion. "Or they think of some other silly thing for us to do?"

The laughter of the two was cut off by a strange, rumbling sound from deep within the volcano. The workers looked at each other with terrified eyes. If the mountain erupted now, they would never be able to get away in time. They stared up at the crater, waiting for the plumes of smoke and ash that would herald their deaths.

None came, though the sound grew louder. Then something emerged from inside the volcano, but far from what they were expecting. It crawled from inside the mountain, its body wreathed in smoke, ash, and flame. It straddled the mouth of the volcano as it rose to its full height, towering over the Matoran and regarding them with eyes of flame.

The giant easily stood 30 feet tall. Its body was equal parts stone and lava, with the solid stone continually melting and reforming. It was something beyond any Matoran's experience, a figure not even found in legend. With a single stride, it would snuff out their lives as if blowing out weakly flickering candles.

"I wondered when you were going to show up, monster!"

The Matoran turned to see that the words had come from Hakann. He was charging up the slope with Avak at his side, both of them ready for battle. The creature opened its mouth and exhaled a jet of flame, but Hakann seemed to shrug it off. He hurled spheres of molten magma at the giant, melting its substance faster than it could recreate it. Angered, it raised its fist, threatening to smash the Matoran into the ground.

Avak shot forward, slamming into the villagers and shoving them out of the way just before the devastating blow landed. Tremors shook the mountain, and cracks shattered the integrity of the lava channels. But none of that mattered to the Matoran just then.

"You saved us," one said to Avak, awe in his voice.

"Don't get used to it," the armored figure replied.

Hakann continued to advance up the mountain, hurling lava and mental bolts at the monster. Amazingly, the giant actually seemed to be giving way. Avak joined his partner, using his pickaxe to tear great chunks of rock out of the creature. Howling with pain, it finally withdrew back into the volcano, where even Hakann could not follow.

Silence descended. One by one, the shaken

Matoran got back to their feet. They looked around anxiously, half expecting the creature to suddenly burst out of the rock beneath their feet. But only Hakann and Avak remained.

"Remember this day, Matoran," Hakann shouted. "If it had not been for us — the Toa of Voya Nui — you would be nothing but ash now. We ask for no reward for our services, only your loyalty and your obedience."

None of the Matoran responded. Avak hurriedly whispered something to Hakann.

"In a short time, Toa Zaktan will reveal a new substance that will ease your burdens and erase your worries," the red Piraka continued. "This will mark the dawn of a new day on Voya Nui. We hope and expect that you will embrace the great opportunity we are giving you, and will turn a deaf ear to any who might want to turn you against us."

The Matoran looked at each other, puzzled. Who would challenge Toa? Especially after they had just proved their heroism by defeating such a frightening beast?

"Depend on us! Listen to us! Obey us!" Hakann bellowed. "And all will be right in your little world!"

A lone Matoran began to clap. Then all the rest joined in, until the canyon echoed with resounding cheers.

On a peak overlooking the action, Garan and Balta watched. They were not cheering.

"Nothing like that ever appeared on Voya Nui before our 'guests' came," Garan said, "and I've never heard of Toa demanding obedience before. How about you?"

Balta didn't reply. His thoughts were with Dalu, who was slowly recovering back in the cave. He knew Velika was keeping watch over her, but he would have felt better if he were there himself.

"They're leaving," Garan said, pointing to Hakann and Avak. "We should follow."

The two Matoran made their way as rapidly as they could over the treacherous slopes. Fortunately, their quarry seemed to be in no hurry. Once well away from the volcano, the two "Toa" stopped, unaware that they were being spied on from the rocks above.

"You overdid," said Avak.

"They needed a grand event," Hakann replied. "I gave them one."

"Next time, tell me when you are going to make the creature slam his fist down. I almost didn't dodge in time."

"No one told you to dive underneath it, you imbecile."

"And if I hadn't, your 'grand event' would have played out for dead witnesses," Avak snapped. "The point was to keep them *alive* so they could spread the word about their heroes, remember?"

Hakann sighed. "Someday, I will figure out why our elemental powers only work in combination. Oh, lava spheres are all right in their place, but they are nothing compared to what I can do when with another Piraka. Think what I could do with the power of pure flame at my command."

The two started walking back toward the

stronghold. "I have," Avak answered. "It keeps me up at night."

It was all a sham, thought Garan as he watched them depart. They manufactured a monster and then defeated it to convince us they are Toa. But how do we convince the rest of the settlement? And more important — what is this "new substance" they talked about?

Zaktan gazed at the small, round piece of crystal he held in his hand. It looked like an exact replica in miniature of the massive crystal sphere in the chamber. Reidak or Vezok would have dismissed it as a bauble and ground it under their heel, never realizing that it and others like it were the key to domination of Voya Nui.

Slowly, almost reverently, he moved the small glass sphere toward the larger crystal. When the two met, the surfaces of both turned immaterial, allowing the smaller crystal to pass through unharmed. When Zaktan withdrew his hand, the sphere contained a small portion of the larger crystal's black and green liquid. A moment later, the sphere changed to a solid color and its contents were no longer visible.

Zaktan picked up one of the launchers Avak had designed. In one swift motion, he loaded the sphere into the launcher. Now prepared, he sent a small portion of his substance underneath the chamber door to summon Reidak and their reluctant guest.

The black Piraka entered the room a moment later, dragging a Ta-Matoran behind him. Reidak stopped well away from the crystal sphere, having found that getting too close to it made him feel disoriented and ill. This particular Matoran had been assigned a resource gathering mission by Hakann, which would take him deep into the mountains, ensuring that he would not be missed by his comrades.

"Hold him still," Zaktan ordered, taking aim with the launcher. He triggered the mechanism, and it hurled the small zamor sphere at the Matoran, striking him dead-on. The sphere turned immaterial once more and passed into the Matoran's body before releasing its contents.

One moment, the Matoran's eyes were filled with fear. The next, they glowed with a sickly crimson light as the virus took effect. Zaktan signaled for Reidak to release his hold. The Matoran made no effort to run, just stood there, his breathing ragged and his body stiff.

Zaktan walked to a far corner of the chamber and pulled on a chain. A small portion of the floor slid away to reveal a pool of molten lava. "Come here."

The Matoran dutifully shuffled to the edge of the pit. His eyes were fixed straight ahead, seemingly oblivious to the burning doom before him.

"Walk into the pit," Zaktan ordered.

Nodding, the Matoran took a step off the edge. His right foot dangled in midair above the boiling pool. Just as he was about to topple in, Zaktan grabbed his arm and flung him back to the center of the room. The Matoran immediately rose and started for the pool again, halting only when Zaktan shouted, "Stop!"

Reidak walked warily around the blank-eyed

Matoran, now standing frozen in place. "What did you do to him?"

"I did nothing," replied Zaktan. "But the contents of that crystal sphere . . . that has delivered this island into our hands. No more worries about Matoran stumbling upon our plans, or hesitating to carry out the dangerous work we require. Now they will be perfect, obedient slaves, with no want and no fear. They will labor until they die, Reidak, at my command."

The black Piraka could not help but catch that Zaktan said "my command" and not "our command." Worse, he knew it was no slip of the tongue. As long as Zaktan was the only one who could get close enough to the sphere to create ammunition for the launchers, he was in a position of power.

Reidak took two steps toward the huge sphere, and stopped. Pain struck him in waves, as if something in that sphere was trying to override his mind and spirit. It was too strong to fight, but he knew surrendering would be his last free act. He had no choice but to back away. The other Piraka had already told him of similar experiences. None of them understood why Zaktan seemed immune to the bizarre effect.

The green Piraka turned his attention back to the Matoran. "You will return to the settlement," he ordered. "You will behave normally. You will see to it that all other Matoran are gathered in the center of the village at sunset. Do you understand?"

The Ta-Matoran nodded and turned away. He would return home and carry out his commands. Nothing would stop him.

Zaktan turned to Reidak. "Alert the others. Have them come here before sunset to claim their launchers and gather a supply of zamor spheres. By the rising of the moon, every Matoran on this island will exist for but one purpose — to find the Kanohi Mask of Life for the Piraka."

Dalu stirred and opened her eyes. She was lying on the hard stone floor of the cave, a blanket of reeds loosely covering her. Her friends looked down at her with concerned eyes.

"See?" Garan said to Balta, quietly. "I told you she would be all right."

"There is nothing funny about a Muaka at midnight," Velika said, as if imparting the wisdom of the ages.

Kazi shot him a hard look. "Okay, now that one just made *no* sense at all."

"He's trying to say she scared us," Garan said. He turned back to Dalu. "And you did. Which one was it?"

"Avak," she replied, struggling to sit up. "I had to, or he would have found you."

"You definitely did the right thing," Garan assured her.

"You did the *brave* thing," Balta added.

"Of what use is the roof against the rains," said Velika, "if there are no walls to stem the flood?"

"That does it," Kazi snapped, starting for the cave mouth. "If anyone wants me, I'll be back at the village where they don't speak in riddles."

"He has a point," said Balta.

"On top of his head," Kazi replied.

"Dalu's sacrifice means nothing if we don't stop them from doing . . . whatever it is they are here to do," said Balta. "And I, for one, don't intend to allow what she did to go to waste. How about you?"

Before Kazi could reply, Piruk burst into the cave. "Garan! The others!"

"What is it?"

"One of the Ta-Matoran, Dezalk, he's gathered them all in the center of the settlement," Piruk said, barely getting the words out. "He says it has something to do with the Toa!"

Garan pondered all of two seconds before coming to a decision. "All right. Dalu will be safe here while the rest of us go check this out."

"We'll all go," said Dalu, back on her feet. "If there's going to be a fight, I'm not missing out."

"If we're lucky, there will be a fight," said Garan as he led them out of the cave. "If we're not, there will be a slaughter."

SIX

The Matoran stood in the heart of their settlement in the twilight. They had gathered here with the understanding that something momentous connected to the Toa was about to happen, and they would be privileged to witness it. Now, after a few minutes of standing and waiting, some began to fidget, others to pace, and still more to scan the surrounding cliffs for some sign of their heroes.

Torches were lit. Small groups began to converse. At first, the tone was puzzled and a bit worried. Where were the Toa? Had something happened to them? For that matter, where was Dezalk? This had been his idea. Angrier voices started to be heard.

"Was this supposed to be a joke?"

"The Toa are probably never coming. It was all a lie."

"Wait until I see Dezalk again —"

Then, as if someone had thrown a switch, all talking ceased. One Matoran pointed up toward the south slope, indicating something that so far only he could spot. And then the waiting was over.

Six Piraka, each armed with a launcher, advanced toward the Matoran from six different directions. They said nothing, only smiled. The reflections of torchlight turned their armor red and gold, but they were not the pure, clean colors of a Toa of Fire — no, they were the fearsome hues of creatures from the pit. Shadows slithered like snakes over their faces and bodies, obscuring their expressions, with the exception of those ever-present, malevolent grins.

Before any of the villagers could cry out, Zaktan fired his launcher. The sphere flew rapidly through the air, struck a Ko-Matoran, and passed into his body. Now the others began to fire and the Matoran panicked, looking desperately for a place to flee. The high rock walls around the settlement had been meant to keep enemies out. On this terrible night, they served only to trap the Matoran inside with six monsters who lurched from the darkness, sowing fear and despair.

There was nowhere to run. Foolishly, the Matoran bunched together, making themselves easier targets. Those who were struck stood straight and still, waiting for orders. Hakann amused himself by sending some of the enslaved Matoran to capture and hold others long enough for his launcher to do its work.

A gust of wind swept through the village, extinguishing the flames of the torches. The settlement was plunged into darkness, punctuated only by the cries of the Matoran and the dull, awful sound of spheres being launched . . . and launched . . . and launched.

By the time Garan and the others reached the settlement, it was all over. The village was empty. By the light of their torches, the Matoran could see the smashed statuary, the damaged suva shrine, and other evidence of the panic that had preceded their arrival. Of their friends, there was no sign at all.

Piruk heard a moan. He turned to see Dezalk slowly getting to his feet. The Ta-Matoran shook his head as if trying to recover his bearings. Then without so much as a glance to left or right, he began to march out of the village. Balta immediately put himself in Dezalk's path.

"Where are the others? What happened?" he yelled.

Dezalk's dead, crimson eyes stared straight ahead. He kept trying to walk forward. When he finally realized someone was blocking his path, he snarled and tried to shove Balta aside. The two Ta-Matoran traded blows while the others watched, too stunned by events to move.

It was Garan who finally said, "Let him go."

"Are you crazy?" asked Balta, struggling to keep his former friend from breaking away. "He may be the only one who knows what's going on!"

"All the more reason to let him escape," said Dalu. "He has some destination in mind. It's probably where the others are, and whoever did . . . whatever . . . to them."

"I don't think it's any secret who did this," said Garan. "The question is, what do we do about it?"

Reluctantly, Balta stepped aside. Dezalk walked swiftly out of the settlement with the six Matoran trailing behind him. They made no effort to conceal themselves, and he seemed to take no notice that they were there. Dezalk traversed narrow rock ledges and made next-to-impossible leaps without any hesitation. Whatever had possessed him had removed any trace of caution or fear.

It was not a long journey; it ended at the base of the volcano. Flickering torches dotted the slopes, where hundreds of Matoran were hard at work. Most were swinging digging tools, carving out holes in the sides of the mountain for lava to flow through. The air was filled with the stench of burning rock and the sound of picks striking stone in unison. Dezalk walked calmly ahead, stepped over a lava flow, grabbed a tool of his own, and went to work.

Dalu started forward. Balta stopped her. "Wait," he whispered. "Look."

Then she saw them. The six beings who had called themselves Toa were standing on a slope nearby, watching the Matoran labor. Their smiles made her sick.

"Slaves," growled Dalu. "They have made them slaves!"

"And all to drain lava from the mountain," muttered Garan. "Why?"

"They're collecting it," said Kazi. "Maybe they are going to use the hot magma for some weapon?"

Garan shrugged. It seemed too obvious somehow. If all they had wanted was lava, there was plenty already present on the surface of the island. There was no need for hundreds of Matoran to dig it out.

He looked at Velika. The Po-Matoran had a way of looking at the world from his own strange viewpoint, sometimes seeing truths that the others missed. Velika was watching the activity with his head cocked slightly to one side, as if listening to a voice only he could hear. When he noticed Garan looking at him, he nodded and smiled.

"He who would empty a lake of fire must have a long spoon," he said.

Well, of course, thought Garan. *You couldn't get too close, so you needed a tool that let you remain at distance — that is what the Matoran are, in this case. It only made sense if you wanted to empty —*

"That's it!" Garan said, keeping his voice down only with great effort. "It has to be." He looked at the others. "Don't you see? It's not the lava they want. They are emptying the volcano! They are after something inside, hidden beneath the lava pool."

"And the only way to get at it is to drain the pool," Balta replied. "So we know 'why,' but not 'what.'"

A Matoran working up near the crater suddenly stumbled on a rock and fell into the volcano.

He never screamed. The only sound was the sizzle of molten lava from inside the mountain. None of the enslaved Matoran even looked up from their labors to mark his passing.

"Nothing could be worth this," Garan said grimly. "Nothing."

"It was all worth it," exulted Hakann. "All the risks, all the hard work —"

"Funny," muttered Vezok. "I don't recall you doing much work."

"This is not a time to bicker," interjected Zaktan. He gestured toward the sea of Matoran, now laboring to advance the Piraka's ambitions. "Not when you remember how far we have come."

Vezok had to admit their leader, whatever his shortcomings, was right. It had not been so very long ago that they were just six more Dark Hunters, taking what missions they could and never seeing any of the rewards. Then Hakann got word of something happening up north, near the ruins of Metru Nui. The six of them made the journey on their own, without informing their superiors. They knew well that such an offense by a Dark Hunter was punishable by death.

By the time they reached the dead City of Legends, whatever had been going on was over with. The city looked no different, but Zaktan noticed a shattered gateway in the Great Barrier. It was he who found the remnants of Makuta's armor, though there was no sign of any body. The others joined him in searching the area, but then something happened. Vezok was not sure what, but it seemed like all of them got the same idea at the same time. There was a Mask of Life out in the world somewhere — and they had to find it. Its energies would make them powerful beyond imagining. Intrigued by the possibilities, they decided then and there to abandon their lives as Dark Hunters. They would be independent and serve only themselves — they would be Piraka.

"The Mask of Life will soon be ours," Zaktan continued. "With the Matoran subdued, there is no one on this island who can stop us."

"Not now," agreed Avak. "But the universe does not end on the shores of this island. There are Matoran here, and a Mask of Power — and where you have those two, can Toa be far behind?"

Lewa Nuva's arrival on Voya Nui began with a pleasant surprise: He was still in one piece.

Back when he had first emerged from his canister on the island of Mata Nui, one arm and both legs had disconnected from his torso. Precious moments had to be spent on reassembling himself, an annoying and not altogether comfortable task. Turaga Vakama had assured the Toa Nuva that would not happen after this journey.

"From everything we have gathered, you spent many, many years floating in the ocean before coming to Mata Nui," he had explained. "We believe that in that time your organic tissue began to decay. By fusing your mechanical components back together upon arrival, you grew new tissue to connect them. Assuming your

canisters don't malfunction, you won't be travel-
ing near long enough for that to happen again."

Lewa twisted the handle and opened his
canister. He crawled out onto an icy shore, got
to his feet, and stretched out the kinks in his
muscles. The others were emerging from their
canisters as well. Onua Nuva was already scouting the area, taking advantage of being the only
Toa who saw well in the dark.

"Nice place," he said flatly. "If you're a goat,
that is. I see nothing but rock for kio around."

Kopaka Nuva extended the telescopic
lense in his mask. "East," he said. "Torches.
Matoran, I think, though they look different from
the ones we know. And what appears to be an
active volcano."

"Then we start looking for the Mask of Life
there," Tahu Nuva announced.

"Why?" asked Gali.

"Don't you know?" Tahu replied, chuck-
ling. "True treasures are *always* found near lava.
Look at me."

Pohatu Nuva smiled. "Not to mention that all that hot air inflates their heads."

Laughing gently, the six Toa Nuva began their long walk toward the volcano and what they hoped was the end of their quest.

"We have three choices," said Garan, looking around at his five companions. "We can run and hope to find a way off this island, maybe find help somewhere else. We can hide in the western mountains, where no one ever goes. Or we can fight, and probably die ... if we don't wind up slaves like our friends."

"The rest of you can do what you want," said Dalu. "I'm fighting."

"Me, too," said Balta. "We haven't survived here this long to just give up."

"The movement of a single pebble can bring down a storm of rock," Velika said, smiling.

Kazi nodded. "Even I get that one. And I'm with them."

Garan looked at Piruk. "No one will think

any less of you if you want to go for help, Piruk. What we are proposing here is suicidal, and there's no reason you have to join us and die, too."

Piruk scraped his shredder claws against each other, sharpening the blades. It was a nervous habit he'd had for years, but this time he seemed to be doing it for a purpose. When he looked up at Garan, there was steel in his gaze.

"Yes," he said. "Yes, there is a reason. You're my friends, and this is my home. If those things are not worth fighting and dying for, then what is?"

"It's settled then," said Garan. "We may be doomed to fall, but before we do, we'll give our enemies reason to regret the day they set foot here. Let's show them you don't have to be a Toa to be a hero."

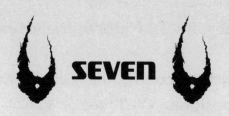

SEVEN

From a perch high above the Piraka, the six Matoran prepared their first strike. Two of the enemies, Reidak and Hakann, had already departed, heading west. This was fine as far as Garan was concerned — the fewer obstacles to this operation, the better.

"Vezok put his launcher down," he said to Balta. "Get down there and grab it. If you can't, at least make sure you get one of those spheres. My guess is they have something to do with what happened to our friends. If we can capture one, maybe we can figure out what it is and how to undo what it's done."

Balta nodded and disappeared into the night. Garan mentally counted down the seconds. If everything went as planned, Balta would be there and back with no problem. If something went wrong, his Ta-Matoran friend was as good as dead.

"Thirty seconds," he said to the others. "Get in position. We'll see if Velika was right about that pebble."

"Garan, look!" said Kazi. "To the west — are those fire bolts?"

Down below, Zaktan was asking the same question. Avak's eyes glowed as his telescopic vision focused on the scene in the distance. After a moment, he shook his head.

"You're not going to like it," he reported. "We have company. And thanks to Reidak being careless about where he throws his boulders, they know we're here."

Zaktan didn't need to be able to see the sight for himself to know what Avak meant. "Toa," he spat as if the word were poison in his mouth.

"About time," said Vezok. "I was beginning to think we were never going to get any action here."

A rumble sounded above them, rapidly

growing until it sounded like thunder. The Piraka whirled around. A sudden lightning bolt illuminated a huge rockslide heading right for them. The first of the boulders hit an outcropping, bounced, and flew right toward Zaktan. The green Piraka's body separated into its trillion component parts, each flying away from where he had been standing so that the rock passed right through. Then he reformed, anger twisting his features.

"Scatter!" he commanded.

Balta waited until the last possible moment. The boulders were almost on top of him as he darted forward, his eyes fixed on Vezok's launcher. The Piraka were diving for cover, apparently unwilling to gamble that their powers would be enough to stop an avalanche.

The Ta-Matoran reached the launcher just as Vezok realized he had forgotten his weapon. He turned to see Balta stealing it.

The Piraka charged. Balta grabbed one of the spheres and took off up the slope. Once out of the circle of torchlight, the Matoran had the cover of darkness to conceal his flight. Vezok started to pursue, then turned to retrieve his launcher. By the time he got it, Balta was long gone.

Toa and *little Matoran thieves,* he said to himself. *Now* this *is more like it.*

"You idiot! You moron!" Hakann raged. "You stupid, incompetent —"

Reidak grabbed him by the throat and choked his words off. "I *really* don't think you want to finish that sentence."

The two Piraka were crouched behind a huge boulder as fire and ice bolts flew by them. Reidak waited until Hakann's arms started flailing in panic before releasing his hold.

"Now. You were saying . . . ?" the black Piraka snarled.

Hakann coughed violently. "I was saying . . . it was an honest mistake. Anyone could have made it." His apologetic tone differed wildly from the fury in his eyes.

"That's better."

"If I can make a suggestion," Hakann said, as an ice dart chipped off part of the rock by his head. "The next time we see six obvious Toa heading for us, don't start throwing half the mountain at them. You know what they say: An ambush is worth a thousand rocks."

"I never saw Toa with armor like that," said Reidak. "Or weird-looking masks like the ones they're wearing."

"If it walks like a Toa, and throws fireballs like a Toa, it's a Toa," Hakann replied. "But you have a point about their appearance. Who are those guys?"

"I don't know who they are," said Tahu. "We can ask them after they're captured."

"Enough fire and ice will drive them from their hiding place," Kopaka said. "Then we can find out why they attacked us."

Pohatu stepped in between the two Toa Nuva. "Um, they're hiding behind a rock," he said. "Remember me? I'm Pohatu. I do rock."

The Toa Nuva of Stone reached out with

his elemental powers, seeking the planes of the rock and its weakest points. Then, using his control of the molecules of stone, he made the massive boulder fracture and fall apart. Now the Toa Nuva's enemies stood revealed.

"There," said Pohatu, smiling. "Not as flashy as an ice bolt, I guess, but . . ."

"But results are what matter," agreed Kopaka.

The red-armored figure unlimbered a weapon and began hurling balls of molten lava at the assembled Toa Nuva. Tahu stepped out in front of the group, saying, "Oh. Lava. If that's the best they can do, this will be a short fight."

Tahu raised one of his magma swords, prepared to swat the incoming missiles away. As he did so, Hakann's eyes glowed. The Piraka's heat vision struck the ground at Tahu's feet, turning the stone to magma. It was Lewa Nuva who spotted it and grabbed the Toa of Fire's arm, yanking him away from the pool.

"News," said the Toa of Air. "Not going to be a short fight."

The black-armored figure charged down the slope, bellowing. Onua concentrated and sent a column of earth slamming into the oncoming foe, knocking him senseless.

"One down," he announced. "Who wants the red one?"

Gali pointed to the downed Piraka, who was already stirring. "He's getting back up. Is he supposed to do that?"

Onua shook his head. "That was enough force to knock out a Kane-Ra bull. Must have just hit him at the wrong angle."

The Toa Nuva of Earth sent his elemental energy forth again. This time, the hammer of earth was twice the size as before and struck Reidak dead-on. When the dust and dirt had cleared, the black Piraka stood unharmed.

"I know we haven't had a real fight since the Rahkshi, but this is getting ridiculous," Tahu grumbled. "Six of us. Two of them. Let's do this."

*   *   *

Zaktan had ordered the remaining Piraka to split up. Vezok and Thok were to go after the Matoran thief and recover the sphere. Avak was to stay and keep an eye on the Matoran slaves and make sure they kept working. Zaktan himself would go to the aid of Hakann and Reidak.

"Two of us for one Matoran?" complained Vezok. "The fight is down below, not up here."

"That's right," said Thok. "The only six beings with the power to rival ours are down below, and Zaktan is going to confront them. Imagine what would happen if he won them over to his side?"

The idea wormed its way into Vezok's mind, trailing suspicion and anger in its wake. "We wouldn't have a chance. With six Toa behind him, Zaktan couldn't be stopped. But who are we kidding? No Toa is ever going to ally with him."

"I know that. You know that. But do the Toa know that? We're all on a barren piece of rock in the middle of nowhere, and probably all after the same thing. In a place like this, you find friends where you can."

Vezok stopped climbing and looked at Thok. "So, what are you saying?"

"I'm saying, if the Toa don't demolish Zaktan, maybe we should."

"Avak tried that," answered Vezok. "He got nowhere. And why should I trust you, anyway?"

Thok laughed. "No reason. No reason at all."

It was worse than Zaktan feared. Six Toa . . . no, not just Toa . . .

Toa Nuva.

The green-armored figure paused, puzzled. How had he known that name? And what did it mean?

He decided neither mattered. What was important was getting to the scene of the battle before things went horribly wrong. These Toa were no doubt on the island to retrieve the Mask of Life for themselves, and that had to be prevented.

He started forward, then stopped again. There was, in fact, very real doubt about why these Toa were here. After all, hadn't the legendary Nidhiki been a Toa before defecting to the Dark Hunters? What if an entire team of Toa had somehow been recruited by that organization and sent to Voya Nui after the Piraka?

Or after me, Zaktan thought darkly. *Of course. One of the Piraka — Hakann or Avak, most likely — made a deal with the Dark Hunters. They would get me, and maybe the others as well, and the traitor in our midst would escape with the Mask of Life.*

Zaktan resumed his journey, this time walking a bit more slowly. His course of action was clear. If the Toa Nuva were working for the Dark Hunters, they would need to be captured and interrogated to find out how much they knew and which Piraka, if any, they were working with.

If, on the other hand, the Toa Nuva were only here to get their hands on the Mask of Life, everything was much simpler. They would just have to die.

Zaktan continued down the slope, trying to decide which choice he liked better.

Lewa Nuva stood, feet planted firmly on the mountainside, air katana gleaming in the moonlight. Facing him was Reidak, who did not seem to be capable of any other expression but a vicious smile.

"Why don't you make things ever-easy and surrender?" offered Lewa. "We are Toa Nuva, after all. We quick-defeated the Rahkshi, so —"

"Rahkshi, huh?" said Reidak. Then, moving so swiftly Lewa could not react, he snatched one of the Toa's air katana and snapped it over his knee. "I pick my teeth with Rahkshi."

Pohatu Nuva triggered his Mask of Speed and raced toward the black Piraka so fast he was a blur. Just as he got close enough to tackle his enemy, Reidak lashed out with a backhand slap and sent the Toa Nuva of Stone tumbling back down the rocky hillside.

A sudden burst of flame blinded the Piraka. When his vision cleared, he saw Tahu, Kopaka, Gali, Onua, and Lewa all closing in on him. He glanced behind, looking for Hakann, but his teammate was gone.

"All right," Reidak grumbled, turning back to the Toa Nuva. "Who wants to die first?"

Zaktan met the red Piraka halfway up the slope. "What are you doing?" asked the Piraka leader. "Where is Reidak?"

"Let's say we need to do one less division of the spoils from this expedition," Hakann replied. "Last I saw, the big idiot was surrounded by Toa, and good riddance."

"Shall I guess?" Zaktan hissed. "He attacked the Toa for no reason. He charged into their midst when a sane being would have held back. Reidak almost begged to be captured, didn't he?"

Hakann's smile faded. "How did you know?"

"Because if I were planning to betray my

partners to a team of Toa," Zaktan snapped, "it's just what I would have done."

Reidak had been utterly defeated.

In fact, he had been utterly defeated so often, Tahu Nuva had lost count. But each time, the Piraka got back up again, stronger than before. Worse, he never seemed to grow tired. If anything, he appeared to be more and more amused.

All six Toa, individually, had brought him down, only to find their powers ineffective during his next attack. There was still the option of using their powers in combination, but if Reidak were to rise again after that and be immune to it . . . the thought wasn't a pleasant one.

Tahu's thoughts suddenly went back to another battle on a volcano, when the opponent had been the mountain itself. It would be a tough trick to pull off, but it might work. Hurriedly, he whispered his plan to Pohatu, Onua, and Lewa.

At the Toa of Fire's signal, Pohatu grabbed Onua and called on the power of the Mask of Speed. Even as he did so, Onua triggered the power of his own Mask of Strength. Pohatu began running rapidly in circles around Reidak as Onua used his hand to slice through the rocky slope. Once the section of ground on which the Piraka stood was cut loose, Lewa used his elemental power of air to catapult both it and Reidak high into the air. At the apex of the flight, the Toa of Air abruptly cut off the flow of his power, sending Piraka and rock plunging to earth.

The impact was so great it shook the mountainside. Rock dust filled the air, making it difficult for even Onua to see. And then the Toa Nuva heard it — a sound coming from the crater more chilling than a Rahkshi's hiss or the chittering of a Bohrok.

Reidak was laughing.

"You know, come to deep-think of it," said Lewa Nuva, looking at his shaken partners. "The island of Mata Nui was not really so bad. Think we could go back?"

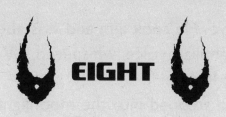

EIGHT

Garan and his team of Matoran had taken refuge beneath a rocky overhang to wait for Balta. They had heard the shouts of their foes and spotted a strange glow on the horizon. At one point, Kazi insisted he had seen one of the false Toa fly straight up into the air and then drop back down again. This was dismissed as ridiculous, since none of the invaders could fly.

The stillness was broken by the harsh sound of metal striking rock. It repeated again and again, coming closer each time. "It's one of them," said Piruk. "It has to be!"

Garan went into a crouch, ready to fire a pulse bolt. He signaled the others to take up positions among the rocks. If they had been trailed by the enemy, they would go down fighting.

A sudden movement up ahead caught

Garan's eye. He took aim and was about to fire when a familiar voice whispered, "Where are you, guys? It's me!"

Balta stepped into the moonlight. He held one of the spheres in his hand. The other Matoran rushed to greet him, but he shook them off. "There's no time," he said. "Thok and Vezok are right behind me. Take the sphere and head for safety."

"Aren't you coming?" asked Dalu.

"Someone has to lead them away from you. I know these rocks. I can lose them and then circle back and find you again."

Dalu looked like she was going to offer to come with him, then thought better of it. Had their positions been reversed, she knew what her answer would have been to such an offer: "I can move faster on my own."

Garan took the sphere. "Be careful," he said. "We'll be heading for —"

Balta cut him off. "Don't tell me."

It took Garan a moment, but then he

understood. What Balta didn't know, the false Toa could not make him tell. The two Matoran shook hands. Then Balta climbed up the rocks and disappeared. Garan started in the opposite direction, the others following. If any of them noticed Dalu's frequent backward glances, they were wise enough not to say.

"How long does it take to track one Matoran?" said Thok.

"Too long," replied Vezok. "Too many places for one to hide. I say we go back, grab one of the others, and bring him to Zaktan. I doubt he can tell one of the little creeps from another."

A small shower of pebbles hit the ground somewhere off to their right. Thok gestured for Vezok to go to the right, while he went left. He slipped around a large outcropping in time to see Balta scrambling up the slope. "Matoran!" he shouted.

Balta looked behind, his eyes meeting

Thok's strangely glowing orbs. The Piraka's spell-binding vision power took hold. The world began to spin around Balta. Unable to keep his balance, he tumbled back down the rocks.

Thok was on top of him in two long strides. The Piraka raised a fist and brought it down. Balta barely managed to get his twin repeller tools up in time. When Thok's blow met the Matoran's tools, the force ricocheted backward, sending the Piraka sprawling.

Balta took off running. He had spotted a cave not far away and hoped it would be deep enough and dark enough to conceal him until the false Toa gave up the chase. Luck was running against him, though, for Vezok spotted him even as he dashed inside.

"He's a small one," the blue Piraka muttered, starting after him. "Might have to throw him back."

Vezok entered the cave, showing unusual caution for a being so powerful. He had heard from Avak how annoying these little Matoran could be. He had no intention of being taken by surprise by one and having to listen to Hakann's mockery for the next few centuries.

It was not a very large cavern and had only a few tunnels branching off it. It took Vezok only a few minutes to search the entire place, but he saw no sign of the Matoran.

For a moment, his mind flashed back to his days as a Dark Hunter. His trainer, Nidhiki, was teaching him how to unlock a vault without leaving any trace. Time and again, Vezok tried and failed, his hands too clumsy for such delicate work. Finally, furious, he had smashed the vault into shards. Nidhiki had wisely declared the test over and passed Vezok.

Direct approach works best, the Piraka said to himself as he exited the cave. Glancing around, he spotted a boulder just the right size. With a mighty heave, he began to roll it toward the cave mouth. Trapping the Matoran inside wouldn't get Zaktan the answers he wanted, but it would keep this particular villager from causing trouble ever again.

Maybe Thok and I can make a little wager,

Vezok thought. *Will the Matoran suffocate before he starves, or starve before he suffocates? And just how long does it take for a Matoran to die?*

Onua Nuva peered over the edge of the crater. Reidak lay at the bottom, battered and bruised, but still smiling. "Had enough?" the Piraka said.

"I think I am supposed to ask *you* that," Onua replied. "What are you, and why are you fighting us?"

"My name is Reidak. I'm a Piraka. Does that name mean anything to you?"

Onua frowned. *Piraka* was a Matoran term, but one that was rarely used. Loosely translated, it meant "thief and murderer," and it was so vile a term that the Matoran considered it an obscenity. The Toa of Earth couldn't imagine why someone would voluntarily brand himself a Piraka.

"Why are you on Voya Nui?" he asked.

"To steal," answered Reidak. "I steal for a living. Oh, and one more thing —"

The Piraka slammed his weapon against the

side of the crater. The ground beneath Onua's feet suddenly turned to quicksand, rapidly dragging the heavy Toa under.

Reidak's grin grew broader. "I kill Toa for fun."

NINE

Gali Nuva was the first to hear the hum. It sounded like a swarm of Nui-Rama in flight, but there was something vaguely more sinister about this sound. By the time the emerald cloud appeared on the horizon, she was already braced for combat.

Pohatu and Lewa ran past her, heading back toward the crater. She thought she heard one of them shouting about Onua sinking into the ground. She glanced to her right and saw Tahu and Kopaka getting into position. Both looked grim, something she could well understand. If two of the enemy could give them such a fight, what if there were three on the island, or more?

The cloud expanded as it flew closer, riveting the attention of all three Toa Nuva. None of them noticed that they were being flanked by the Piraka until a devastating blast of Hakann's mental energy struck Gali. She had been ready for physical combat, but this struck at her mind in a way nothing else ever had. For a split second, it seemed like all of existence had gone black. When awareness returned to her, it felt like her brain had been savaged.

Hakann didn't even bother trying to hide. He fired a half dozen balls of lava in her direction, forcing Gali onto the defensive. But he had underestimated her quickness. Even as she dodged his magma missiles, she was using her elemental energies to conjure a sphere of water around her foe.

The crimson-armored Piraka almost panicked. One moment, he was breathing the arid air of Voya Nui, the next his mouth was full of water. Then his years of experience reasserted themselves — he had, after all, slain Toa of Water before. His eyes glowed as beams of heat vision shot out, converting the sphere of water into steam. Hidden by the billowing cloud, he did a backflip onto a rock and fired his heat vision again, this time at Gali.

The Toa of Water felt the aqua axe in her right hand grow scorching hot. Crying out, she dropped it. Hakann followed up with heat vision on a wide beam, bathing her in molten temperatures. Feeling herself weakening, Gali summoned a cooling rain to try to fend off the heat.

"Fire versus water," Hakann said. "It would seem we are pretty evenly matched. Too bad fire is not the only trick I know."

A second mental bolt, more powerful than the last, lashed out at Gali. With so much of her mental energy devoted to fighting off the heat, she had no way to defend herself. The pain grew in intensity until her consciousness took the only way out and shut down. She collapsed on the ground.

"One down," said the Piraka.

Pohatu and Lewa both grabbed one of Onua's arms and pulled. Their combined strength was enough to free him from the quicksand, but while they were doing that, Reidak climbed out of the crater.

"He's mine," said Lewa, tossing aside his lone remaining air katana.

"Lewa, don't —"

"He's mine!" Lewa repeated, stalking toward the Piraka.

Reidak charged. Lewa sidestepped and darted out a foot, sending his enemy tumbling onto the rocky ground. Reidak rolled over and kept rolling, bowling over the Toa of Air. He tried to follow it up with a blow to the head, but Lewa dodged in time. A sharp kick bought the Toa some space, and a two-handed smash into Reidak's grin sent the Piraka flying.

Lewa advanced as Reidak got up on one knee and spat. "Here I thought you Toa were so peace loving," the Piraka laughed.

"Peace loving," Lewa replied. "Not weak."

Reidak suddenly vaulted forward. Lewa sidestepped again, this time grabbing on to the Piraka's back as he flew by. He hurled his enemy through the air toward Pohatu. The Toa of Stone flipped onto his back and caught the flying Piraka with a kick from his powerful legs. This sent

Reidak hurtling toward Onua. Calling on the Mask of Strength, Onua leapt into the air until he was just slightly higher than the speeding Piraka. Then he brought both fists down in a devastating double blow. Reidak dropped like a rock and smashed into the ground.

Before the Piraka could rise again, Lewa was there pinning him to the ground with one knee while he twisted Reidak's arm behind him. "You broke something of mine," the Toa of Air said. "Maybe I should quick-return the favor?"

Solid stone bands erupted from the ground to bind the Piraka. Lewa looked up at Pohatu, who was pointing up the slope. "Trouble," said the Toa of Stone. "Leave this one. The others need our help."

Avak ducked beneath an ice blast. He had spotted Zaktan and Hakann heading back down this way and decided to join them, orders or not. It wasn't so much that he thought the other Piraka needed his help. He just didn't want to let his "allies" out of his sight for too long.

"Do you know what I did when I first joined the Dark Hunters?" asked Avak, dodging a hail of icicles. "I was a jailer. Other Hunters would bring in captives and I would lock them up."

"You should have saved a cell for yourself," Kopaka Nuva said.

"But there was one problem," Avak said, ignoring the Toa's comment. "Any lock can be picked. Any chain can be snapped. If someone wants to escape from a cell bad enough, they will find a way."

Avak swung his pickaxe, narrowly missing Kopaka's head. The Toa Nuva responded by freezing both weapon and hand. If he expected that to stop the Piraka, though, he was mistaken. Avak smashed his hand against a rock wall and shattered the ice.

"Now where was I?" said the Piraka. "Oh, yes, once I realized no escape-proof cell could be built, I went to the head of the Dark Hunters with the problem. He sent me to the Brotherhood of Makuta, and they . . . did things to me."

Kopaka hurled hailstones the size of

boulders, only to see Avak bat them aside. Then the Piraka paused, as if lost in thought. The next instant, a cage made of flaming bars had sprung into existence around Kopaka.

"Now I make my own cells," Avak finished. "Any kind I need."

Despite the intense heat, Kopaka smiled. Tahu Nuva had tried to imprison him in something similar once, and a fraction of his power had been enough to freeze the flames. He unleashed his elemental energies and a thin sheen of frost formed on the fiery bars. Then it just as quickly melted away. Kopaka tried a second and a third time, only to see his efforts fail.

"I forgot to tell you," said Avak. "The colder you make it in there, the hotter the bars burn. Eventually, you'll use up your power and the heat will finish you off — if the smoke doesn't get you first."

The Piraka grinned as he saw more ice forming on his cell. *This Toa may not know when to give up, but it changes nothing,* he thought. *And that's two down.*

*　　*　　*

Tahu Nuva watched as the green cloud coalesced into a monstrous figure wielding a three-bladed weapon. The two faced each other on a rocky precipice, with the sea roaring far below.

"I may not know who — or what — you are," said Tahu. "But I have seen enough to know you and your allies are what Toa exist to battle."

"Toa," Zaktan said, a harsh laugh echoing in multiple voices. "You are an anachronism — pure and noble heroes, still striving for right in a universe of chaos, unwilling to admit that your day is long over."

"And what is going to replace us? Monsters like you?"

Zaktan nodded and raised his weapon. "We will walk over your bodies, Toa, on our way to a new age."

The Piraka swung his blades. Tahu barely got his twin magma swords up in time to counter the blow. Zaktan pushed him away and then thrust again, forcing Tahu to step back toward the cliff. The Toa of Fire caught Zaktan's weapon between his two swords and sent waves of heat up the blades. But for each fragment of Zaktan's sword that melted, pieces flew from the Piraka's substance to make up the loss.

"It is not so easy as that," Zaktan said. "I am my weapon. My weapon is me. To destroy it, you must first destroy me."

"With pleasure," growled Tahu.

The Toa of Fire advanced now, swinging both his swords, only to find each blow countered by his opponent's weapon. Zaktan moved impossibly fast. The few times Tahu thought he would land a solid hit, his target flew apart and the blade passed harmlessly through.

"That 'body made of multiple little pieces' thing is a neat trick," said Tahu. "Must be lousy when you sneeze, though."

"A problem you will no longer face, Toa" replied the Piraka. "That is, once I have removed your head from your shoulders."

Zaktan made another thrust, this one checked by the power of Tahu's Mask of Shielding. The Piraka laughed. "So you hide behind your force shield? Is this the mighty Toa that villains must quake before? I suppose it is true, then — the Toa with the longest careers are those who master the art of running and hiding."

Tahu's common sense told him he was being baited, and not to respond. But a glance down the slope revealed that Gali and Kopaka had both fallen. The sight filled him with rage and a determination to wipe that sick smile off the Piraka's face. He dropped the shield.

Metal clanged against metal, sparks flying everywhere as the two antagonists traded thrusts and slashes. They were both experienced fighters, both leaders, and neither was willing to concede anything. For Tahu, defeat might mean death. For Zaktan, it would certainly mean rebellion by the other Piraka. Thus, both fought as if it were the last battle they would ever know.

Tahu's two magma swords gave him an advantage, one he did his best to press. But Zaktan's constantly shifting body and his obvious skill with his blades checked the Toa at every turn. Dodging a thrust, Tahu leapt on top of a boulder, only to have Zaktan's next slash split the rock in half. Tahu turned his fall into a maneuver, somersaulting in midair and slamming both feet into the startled Piraka. Zaktan dispersed into a cloud of buzzing, swarming protodites that cut off Tahu's vision. The Toa spun, expecting the Piraka's arm to suddenly materialize, sword in hand, to strike a killing blow.

Instead, the cloud moved away and reformed into his enemy. "You are on the wrong side in this battle," said Zaktan. "Join with me and we will rule all together. We can even free your fellow Toa, provided they agree to serve."

"And what about your allies?"

"Unnecessary, if I have the power of Toa on my side," the Piraka replied, as coldly as if he were discussing stepping on fikou spiders. "I will even give you the honor of disposing of them."

"Why don't I save time and start with you?" said Tahu, charging forward.

Blade clashed with blade once again, while the hungry sea waited to claim the loser. Their weapons locked together, both fighters exerted all their strength to push the other away. It was Zaktan who finally shoved Tahu back, throwing the Toa Nuva slightly off balance. In that instant, Zaktan thrust his blade into a gap in the Toa's armor.

Tahu expected to feel a piercing wound, but what happened instead was far worse. As the blade struck, it disintegrated into millions of protodites who swarmed through his body, attacking his armor and his organic tissue. The pain was searing, overwhelming, and Tahu Nuva could not help but scream. As unconsciousness claimed him, he teetered on the edge of the cliff and fell.

Zaktan reached out and grabbed the Toa's arm. "No, my enemy," the leader of the Piraka hissed. "You do not die so easily. There are still agonies that you have yet to taste."

TEN

Lewa, Onua, and Pohatu were confronted by a horrible sight: In the brief time they had been struggling with Reidak, three of their number had fallen. Worse, their enemies had now been joined by two more, one in white armor and one in blue.

"We need to rescue the others and regroup," said Pohatu. "The power of all six Toa united is needed here."

"And if we fall, too?" asked Onua. "I honor my brothers and my sister above all things . . . but this would be more than just our defeat. The Mask of Life would be lost and the Great Spirit doomed to die."

It was Lewa who made the decision. "If we leave our Toa friends to die, we are not worthy of the trust Mata Nui has placed in us. We quick-save them, if we have to tear these Piraka apart to do it."

A plan was made. At Pohatu's signal, Lewa used his elemental power to create a blinding storm of rock dust. At its height, Pohatu used the Mask of Speed to race toward where Gali lay, while Onua slipped behind Avak. The Toa of Stone grabbed his fallen friend and sped back to Lewa, even as Onua stunned Avak with a surprise blow. Before the Piraka could respond, Onua slammed him with a fist of earth, knocking him unconscious. When he fell, Kopaka's cage disappeared.

"Come on," Onua said to the unconscious Toa Nuva of Ice. "This fight isn't over yet."

The storm abated. Zaktan's eyes narrowed at the sight of how much the Toa Nuva had achieved in only a few seconds. If they succeeded in reviving their two comrades, the Toa would have the edge in numbers again.

"We must strike now," he said. "Use your power, Thok, and eliminate them all."

The white Piraka shook his head. "That much effort would leave me too weak, if there were to be . . . another fight."

Zaktan hurled some of his substance forward, surrounding Thok with bands of protodites. "I was *not* making a request. Do it!"

Thok knew he had no choice, but privately swore he would avenge this humiliation later. For now, the Toa Nuva were all bunched together as they tended to their wounded. That would make things much easier. The Piraka reached out with his power over the inanimate to bring the mountainside to life. Now resembling a stone giant, it towered 50 feet in the air as it lumbered toward the Toa.

The creature's shadow fell over the heroes. Pohatu looked up and knew immediately what he had to do, if there was only time to do it. He would make the Piraka regret choosing stone for their attack. Sending his elemental power forward in waves, he seized control of the giant, shattered it into pieces, and sent the rubble flying toward the assembled Piraka.

Island of Doom

The rocks exploded as they struck the ground, sending Thok, Vezok, and Zaktan scrambling for cover. Hakann chose that moment to strike, blasting Pohatu and Lewa with mental energy and felling them both. That left only Onua still at full strength.

The Toa of Earth stood amongst the bodies of his friends. He had no idea if Tahu, Gali, or the others might already be dead. He knew that even his massive strength could not stop so many foes at once, especially since he could hear Reidak breaking free behind him. And his own words came back to haunt him — wasn't retrieving the Mask of Life what was most important? Shouldn't he escape to fight another day?

He looked down at Gali and the rest, lying so still. Then he glanced up to see Tahu's limp body discarded on the slope like it was worthless trash. These were friends he had fought beside, laughed with, mourned with, now helpless at the hands of their enemies. In that moment, Onua made his decision — he would live or die here, as a Toa Nuva.

Ripping a half ton of rock free from the ground, he hurled it at Zaktan. Before it had even struck home, Onua was running toward his foes, a chilling battle cry escaping from his lips.

He never made it. The powers of Zaktan, Thok, and Hakann struck at him at once, slowing him down but not stopping him. It was left to Vezok to strike the final blow, smashing the Toa of Earth into oblivion.

Zaktan looked around. Reidak and Avak were back on their feet and the others were already moving to loot the bodies of the Toa Nuva. None of them seemed upset at the heroes' defeat, making him wonder if perhaps the Toa had only come to Voya Nui for the Mask of Life. There was no conspiracy against him — not one involving the Toa, at least. And this great victory would surely cement his leadership, at least long enough to retrieve the mask and get off this barren rock.

"They're still alive," reported Vezok. "Even the one I hit."

"Do you want me to cage them?" asked Avak. "Maybe they have information on the mask we can use."

Zaktan smiled. He wondered how many other times these Toa, or others like them, had been defeated and how many other times their enemies had thought to keep them captive. It was a fool's gamble, like taking a refreshing dip in energized protodermis and hoping it wouldn't kill you. The leader of the Piraka would not go down in legend as a fool.

"We have all hunted Toa. We know how dangerous they are, and never more so than when we think they are defeated," he said. "Today, we won the battle, but tomorrow? No. Our quest here is too important to risk interference."

He picked up Tahu and threw him down the slope to lie beside his friends. "Take their Masks of Power and their weapons — we may be able to sell them. Then bring them to the volcano."

"I see," said Hakann. "We will use the launchers and turn them into slave laborers."

"Even enslaved Toa would be a threat," Zaktan replied. "When you have reached the crater of the volcano . . . throw them in and let them burn."

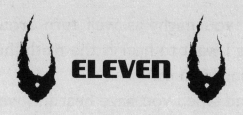

ELEVEN

Jaller sat in the ruins of the Ta-Metru Great Furnace. Many days had passed since he had issued his ultimatum to the Turaga. In that time, no Matoran had lifted a tool to do any work in the city, even to create shelters for themselves. Both Turaga Vakama and Takanuva had come to him to ask that he relent and allow the repairs to Metru Nui to continue. He had refused.

If we are no more than frightened little beings who must be protected — hostages and victims for every foe we encounter — then we are a weakness, he said to himself. *We benefit no one, not the Toa Nuva, not ourselves. I will not let helplessness and fear be the legacy of the Matoran.*

He looked up to see Turaga Nokama approaching. She had gone only a few steps into the rubble of the furnace when Jaller's voice stopped her. "If this is another plea, noble

Nokama, you might as well turn around. The only thing I want to hear is the truth the Turaga are keeping from us."

"And when you have heard it, what then? Will it change anything?" replied Nokama. "You will not be able to do anything with that knowledge but worry and grieve and wish you had never learned any of it. I know that is what I wish."

Jaller was tired. He was not going to make the same argument he had made to Vakama and Dume yet again. "I will do whatever I can do, as a Matoran and as captain of the Ta-Metru Guard."

Nokama sat down on a piece of masonry. "Dume and Vakama do not know I have come. I could have announced it at the top of my lungs and they would not have heard me, so consumed are they with worry. They would not approve of my coming to you, but I believe all beings have a right to know why they are going to die."

Before Jaller could respond, Nokama began her tale. She told him of the discoveries made by

Turaga Dume and Turaga Nuju; of the Great Mask of Life; of Voya Nui; and finally of the Toa Nuva's journey to that island to find the mask and save the Great Spirit. Jaller listened to it all with rapt attention, never speaking until she had finished.

"If Mata Nui dies —" he began.

"Then must not the universe die with him?" said Nokama. "Up to now, the Toa have fought to bring light and hope back to the Matoran. But if they had failed, and Makuta triumphed, at least we would have been alive to nurture a dream of a better future. If they fail this time . . . there will be no future."

"And there has been no word of them?"

"None. Dume believes that if they were going to return, they would be back by now. He fears they are lost. Vakama urges that Takanuva be sent to find them, but Dume insists the Toa of Light is needed here. I cannot imagine the reason for that, but we must respect his wisdom."

Jaller frowned. "Are you certain it really *is* Turaga Dume?" He remembered well the story of how the evil Makuta had once taken on Dume's shape in an effort to conquer Metru Nui.

"Onewa has looked into his mind," Nokama answered. "Yes, it is the true Turaga." She paused, then added, "I am sorry to have burdened you with this, Jaller, for there is nothing that can be done. But at least now, when the stars are extinguished and the end comes, you will understand."

Without another word, Turaga Nokama departed, leaving Jaller to ponder her message. The news was devastating, but it did not leave him feeling lost or hopeless. Tahu had always told him that you could not fight a shadow — you had to perceive the shape and substance of your enemy to defeat him. Now he knew what they faced, and that was the first step toward victory.

There is something I can do, he decided. *But I will not tell Takanuva or the Turaga — they would only try to stop me, and every moment matters now.*

He ran from the ruins, plans already forming in his brain. He would need help — the best, most trustworthy, and bravest Matoran he could find — and then they would go to Voya Nui themselves. They would find the Toa Nuva and this Mask of Life, they would help to save the Great Spirit. Somehow, they would make things right.

He didn't fool himself. A journey deemed too dangerous to Toa would probably mean a quick end to Matoran. But he also knew there was no choice. And although he had never met Garan, the same words uttered by that Matoran echoed in his mind now:

You don't have to be a Toa to be a hero.

BrickMaster

Sign up Today for the Ultimate LEGO® Experience!

REWARD A:

Brickmaster exclusive "From the LEGO Vaults" CD-ROM! (A $30 value!)

REWARD B:

Six 36 Page LEGO BrickMaster Magazines including exclusive BIONICLE® content and BIONICLE comics! (A $20 value!)

REWARD C:

Receive LEGO sets by mail every 2 months! (Total value of 5 sets =$20!)

REWARD D:

Two LEGO Shop At Home coupons!

REWARD E:

FREE BONUS LEGOLAND® California child's admission ticket!

#KBM25 LEGO® BrickMaster™
One Year Subscription

Includes Rewards A+B+C are a $70 Value, plus you get Bonus Rewards D & E!

Only $39.99

Check out www.LEGOBrickMaster.com for more details!

Please give the operator this code: SCB25

LEGO club